Dear Parents and Educators,

Welcome to Penguin Young Readers! As parents and educators, you know that each child develops at his or her own pace—in terms of speech, critical thinking, and, of course, reading. Penguin Young Readers recognizes this fact. As a result, each Penguin Young Readers book is assigned a traditional easy-to-read level (1–4) as well as a Guided Reading Level (A–P). Both of these systems will help you choose the right book for your child. Please refer to the back of each book for specific leveling information. Penguin Young Readers features esteemed authors and illustrators, stories about favorite characters, fascinating nonfiction, and more!

Cowboy Roy

LEVEL **2**

GUIDED READING LEVEL **H**

This book is perfect for a **Progressing Reader** who:
- can figure out unknown words by using picture and context clues;
- can recognize beginning, middle, and ending sounds;
- can make and confirm predictions about what will happen in the text; and
- can distinguish between fiction and nonfiction.

Here are some **activities** you can do during and after reading this book:
- Fiction: This story is fiction; it is made-up and is not real. But if Roy were a real cowboy, what could he ride instead of a bike? There are clues in the story—it could buck and throw its rider off its back. It could even have a cool name—just like Silver! What could a real cowboy ride?
- Make Connections: In this story, Roy feels like a "cowbaby" because he can't ride his bike without training wheels and because Jesse and James laugh at him. Think about a time when you felt the way Roy feels. What or who made you feel that way?

Remember, sharing the love of reading with a child is the best gift you can give!

—Bonnie Bader, EdM, and Katie Carella, EdM
    Penguin Young Readers program

*Penguin Young Readers are leveled by independent reviewers applying the standards developed by Irene Fountas and Gay Su Pinnell in *Matching Books to Readers: Using Leveled Books in Guided Reading*, Heinemann, 1999.

To Megan, who helped us remember what
it is like to learn to ride a two-wheel bike—
Love, Mom and Dad

Penguin Young Readers
Published by the Penguin Group
Penguin Group (USA) Inc., 375 Hudson Street, New York, New York 10014, USA
Penguin Group (Canada), 90 Eglinton Avenue East, Suite 700, Toronto, Ontario M4P 2Y3, Canada
(a division of Pearson Penguin Canada Inc.)
Penguin Books Ltd., 80 Strand, London WC2R 0RL, England
Penguin Group Ireland, 25 St. Stephen's Green, Dublin 2, Ireland (a division of Penguin Books Ltd.)
Penguin Group (Australia), 250 Camberwell Road, Camberwell, Victoria 3124, Australia
(a division of Pearson Australia Group Pty. Ltd.)
Penguin Books India Pvt. Ltd., 11 Community Centre, Panchsheel Park, New Delhi—110 017, India
Penguin Group (NZ), 67 Apollo Drive, Rosedale, Auckland 0632, New Zealand
(a division of Pearson New Zealand Ltd.)
Penguin Books (South Africa) (Pty.) Ltd., 24 Sturdee Avenue,
Rosebank, Johannesburg 2196, South Africa

Penguin Books Ltd., Registered Offices: 80 Strand, London WC2R 0RL, England

Library of Congress Control Number: 99089375

ISBN 978-0-448-41568-0                              10 9 8 7 6 5 4 3 2 1

# by Cathy East Dubowski and Mark Dubowski

Penguin Young Readers
An Imprint of Penguin Group (USA) Inc.

Howdy!

My name is Roy.

This is my sister, Meg,

and her doll, Dolly.

We live on the A OK Ranch.

I am a good cowboy.

I can rope.

I can round up strays.

"Get along, little doggie!"

But there is one thing

I cannot do.

I cannot ride

like the other cowboys.

"Look at Jesse and James!" I say.

Meg says, "I don't like them.

They are not nice cowboys."

"Maybe so," I say.

"But they sure can ride!"

I go to the barn.

There is my new bike.

I wish I could ride it.

I call my bike Silver.

It is the best bike

in the West!

I will try again to ride.

I hop on Silver.

Silver bucks and bucks.

Then Silver throws me off.

Shucks!

So my dad puts on

some training wheels.

Meg says, "Try again, Roy.

You can do it!"

I try again.

I *can* ride

with the training wheels.

But do I feel like a cowboy?

No!

I feel like a cowbaby!

Uh-oh.

Here come Jesse and James.

"Look at Roy," says Jesse.

"He can't ride the real way."

"What a baby!" says James.

"Don't make fun of my brother!"

Meg yells.

Jesse and James laugh.

Then they ride away.

"Don't feel bad," Meg tells me.

But I do.

The next day I take off

my training wheels.

I don't want to look like a baby.

I want to ride like a cowboy.

Meg and I head up to Dry Gulch.

She helps me get on my bike.

And she helps me get up

each time I fall!

Oh no!

Look who came back.

Jesse and James.

What are they up to?

I know one thing.

They are up to no good!

Jesse and James grab Dolly.

"Stop!" Meg yells.

"Stop!" I yell, too.

But Jesse and James

do not give Dolly back.

"We are outlaws!" says Jesse.

"Your doll is coming with us!"

says James.

They laugh and ride off.

Meg starts to cry.

"Don't worry," I tell her.

"We can catch them."

But Jesse and James

are too fast for us.

There is only one way

to catch Jesse and James.

I hop on Silver.

I take a deep breath.

I shout, "Giddy-up, Silver!"

I roll fast down the hill.

Silver bucks and bucks.

But I hang on.

This time I do not fall off.

I am riding like a cowboy!

Yee-haw!

I catch up with Jesse and James.

Yikes! I cannot stop!

I crash into Jesse and James!

But I catch Dolly.

Jesse and James are crying

like cowbabies.

They head for the hills.

Silver and I look

for my sister.

"Meg!" I shout.

"I can ride!"

I give Meg back her doll.

"Oh, thank you, Roy!" she says.

"You are the best cowboy

in the West!"

I pat Silver.

I know how to make

Silver go.

Now I just need to learn

how to make him stop!